# HOW SPIDER STOPPED THE LITTERBUGS

ROBERT by KRAUS

## SCHOLASTIC INC.
New York  Toronto  London  Auckland  Sydney

FOR
PARKER
+ the
BAKERSFIELD, CA.
SCHOOL
BOYS + GIRLS

ISBN 0-590-44462-X

Copyright © 1991 by Robert Kraus.
All rights reserved. Published by Scholastic Inc.

12 11 10 9 8 7 6 5 4 3 2 1    1 2 3 4 5 6/9

Printed in the U.S.A.        24

First Scholastic printing, April 1991

I was all excited!
It was the day of the big school picnic.
I brought my lunchbox, my umbrella, and my guitar.

On the way to school I met my two friends, Fly and Ladybug.
Ladybug had her trumpet, and Fly had his drum.
I knew we were going to have lots of fun.

"Looks like rain," muttered Fly.
"I hope it doesn't rain on our picnic," said Ladybug.
"Don't worry, Ladybug," I said. "I brought an umbrella."

We met Miss Quito and the rest of the schoolbugs in front of the school.
Miss Quito counted bugs.
"There are two bugs missing," she said.
"Let's go, anyway," said Fly.

Just then two voices cried, "Wait! Don't leave
without us!"
It was the twin caterpillars.
They'd overslept.

"I was hoping the Litterbugs would come back to school for the picnic," said Ladybug.

"Fat chance," Fly said. "They're first-grade dropouts."
We all held hands and walked over to Bugg Park.

When we saw the park, we gasped.
It was a mess!
"What a dump," said Fly.

Someone had overturned all the trash baskets.
There were bottles, cans, and newspapers all over —
not to mention banana peels and apple cores.

A note carved in a tree read,
"The Litterbugs were here!"
"I should have known it was them," grumbled Fly.
"Our picnic is ruined!" cried Ladybug.

"Let's go home," said Fly.
"Wait a minute!" I said.

"The Litterbugs made this mess, but we can clean it up!
Nobody's going to litter on *our* picnic!"

Soon the park was so clean you could eat off the grass. In fact, Spider did just that.

"Hooray!" said Ladybug.
"Don't hooray too soon," said Fly. "Look who's here!"

"HERE COME THE LITTERBUGS!"

They swarmed! They swooped!
They jumped! They *dumped*!
One Litterbug even kicked dirt in Fly's face!

"They're not only Litterbugs, they're bullies," cried Fly.
I remembered what I had done to the bullies last
Halloween. But I didn't have my pumpkin disguise
with me.

Then I thought of an old saying: "Music hath charms to soothe the savage bug!"

"Come on, Ladybug and Fly," I said. "We're going to play a little rock and roll!"

I started singing.
*Come on bugs.*
*Let's rock and roll.*
*Don't litter, litter, litter.*
*Just jitter, jitter, jitter,*
*All day long.*

It was unbelievable!
First the Litterbugs stopped dumping.
Then they started shaking. Soon they were dancing!
They'd dropped their litter and started to jitter.

The Litterbugs had changed into jitterbugs!

We had a great picnic after all.
And when it was over, the Litterbugs even helped clean up.

"Jittering is more fun than littering!" said
Lenny Litterbug.

"You did it again, Spider," said Ladybug.
"I couldn't have done it without you guys," I said.
"You bet," said Fly.

The End

HI, KIDS + BUGS,
1. PLease Don't LITTER!
2. PUT ALL LITTER IN A LITTER BASKET.
3. RECYCLE BOTTLES, NEWSPAPERS AND TIN CANS.
4. GARBAGE WON'T GO AWAY.
Bee LIKE me.
YOUR friend
SPIDER
SAVE OUR EART